Beagle in Trouble
Super Sleuth II

Beagle in Trouble
Super Sleuth II

Twelve Solve-It-Yourself Mysteries

 by Jackie Vivelo

Troll Associates

A TROLL BOOK, published by Troll Associates

Published by arrangement with G.P. Putnam's Sons, a division of The Putnam Publishing Group. For information address G.P. Putnam's Sons, a division of The Putnam Publishing Group, 200 Madison Avenue, New York, New York 10016.

First Troll Printing, 1989

Printed in the United States of America.

10 9 8 7 6 5 4 3 2

ISBN 0-8167-1548-3

To AJV

Contents

Beagle in Trouble

Super Sleuth II

The Labor Day Arson Mystery

■ **1** ■

The last week before school starts is the worst time of the whole year. It's still summer but it might as well not be. On the Friday before Labor Day, I was sitting around wondering who my homeroom teacher would be, thinking about the kids I hadn't seen all summer, and wishing the only kid my age in the neighborhood hadn't gone away with his parents. Charles Beaghley isn't exactly what I'd call a friend. "Beagle" is more like a last resort. But he and I are partners in a detective agency, and I guess I miss the mysteries as much as I miss him.

Of course, the weekend before school starts is not the best time to go looking for a mystery. Besides, there was a sign nailed across the door of the shed

11

we use for our detective agency that said:

CLOSED UNTIL SEPTEMBER

Beagle and I had spent part of the summer working as detectives and part of it fishing at Wildwood Lake, following trails in Taylor's Woods, and catching crayfish in Turtle Creek. When Beagle left for Washington state with his parents, he brought his crayfish over for me to take care of while he was away. We had kept one each out of the dozen or so we had caught.

I tried putting his crayfish in the tank with my crayfish, but the two of them started racing around and jumping when they got near each other. When the orange color on their claws began to spread and get brighter, I put Beagle's crayfish into a bowl by itself. Also, the only thing those two crayfish liked to eat was baked chicken, which was making them unpopular with my mom. Now I wished I could drop them both back into the creek, but I decided I'd better tell Beagle first.

Hoping he was back home, I walked past Beagle's house and decided to look at the shed we use for an office. *He has to come home sometime,* I thought.

Something had changed. The sign Beagle had nailed across the door was gone. The black squiggles Beagle had painted during the summer gleamed on the door:

12

THE BEAGLE DETECTIVE AGENCY
Ellen Sloan, *Super Sleuth*   Charles Beaghley, *Owner*

As I was staring at the door, it opened, and Beagle stuck his head out.

"Hey, Ellen, I just tried calling you. There's a case we have to solve."

It figured. He probably hadn't been home an hour, and he had already found a mystery. Beagle just seems to attract trouble.

"What happened?" I asked.

"Two of the buildings on the fairgrounds burned down night before last."

"I heard about it, but what kind of case is that?" I asked.

"Well, you know my dad's one of the fairgrounds administrators, and he has just been talking to the police. They found evidence that someone set those fires. It's a case of arson."

"Do you think we should let the police handle this?"

"If it weren't for my dad, I would. But Ellen, I'd like to help him, and I think you and I can solve this thing faster than the police can. Come on in, and I'll tell you why."

The reason Beagle thought we could solve the mystery was that he has been wandering through the fairgrounds for most of his life and knows all the employees.

"As soon as Dad heard it was arson, he suggested the fires might have been set by one of the men who were fired a few days ago. Two of them were fired for laziness, another one had been stealing equipment, and another man's carelessness caused some property damage. All of the men were angry at being fired and a couple of them even made some threats. At the time, Dad didn't think that they really meant to make trouble, but the fire changed his mind."

"How are we going to find clues?" I asked.

"Easy," Beagle said. "Tomorrow all the people connected with the fairgrounds will be at a picnic. Come with us, and you and I will collect information."

One thing I never doubt is Beagle's ability to get people to talk to him. So Labor Day found us mingling with the fairgrounds employees and talking about the four men who had been fired. Mr. Beaghley had told us that their names were Ron Vernack, Larry Russell, Mike Noggle, and Jake Lalic. By mid-afternoon we had heard a lot of things that were no help at all and a few things that might help. It quickly became obvious that Mr. Beaghley was right: One of the men he had named had set the fire. Apparently one of the other three had acted as lookout.

From all the information we gathered during the discussions with employees, we made a list of the most helpful comments. The clues were:

1. The day the men were fired, Larry tried to persuade the man who later acted as lookout to go to Nebraska with him, where Larry thought they could work with his brother. The lookout, who is known to dislike Larry, refused.
2. Ron and Jake had been playing poker with the lookout during working hours until their supervisor found out.
3. Jake and the arsonist had a serious argument that almost turned into a fight.
4. The lookout is said to be the only person who likes the arsonist, but everyone else is too frightened to give him away.

Below the clues I had written in my notebook, I drew up a chart like this:

	lookout	arsonist
RON		
LARRY		
MIKE		
JAKE		

"So, what does the first clue tell us?" I asked Beagle, who's better at finding clues than at deciding what they mean.

"Well, Larry isn't the lookout. He isn't even a friend of the lookout."

"Okay, so let's mark him off the list under the heading *lookout*."

[Can you solve the mystery and find out which of the men is the lookout and which one is the arsonist? Try finding the lookout first. Remember you may need to go over the clues more than once. When you think you know the answer, read Beagle and Ellen's solution on the next page.]

Solution to "The Labor Day Arson Mystery":

As Beagle said, clue #1 shows that Larry is not the lookout. Neither is Ron or Jake, according to clue #2. So, the lookout is Mike. Since the lookout did not actually set the fires, Mike is not the arsonist.

Clue #3 reveals that Jake was not the arsonist. Clue #1 says that the lookout does not like Larry but, according to clue #4, the lookout does like the arsonist, so Larry is not the arsonist. The arsonist, therefore, is Ron Vernack.

Mr. Beaghley phoned to tell the police what we had found out. By the end of the day, with the mystery solved, we settled down to eat barbecued chicken, hamburgers, potato salad, macaroni salad, potato chips, corn chips, hard-boiled eggs, cherries, plums, peaches, nectarines, watermelon, and lots more.

I had just decided I never wanted to see any more food, when Mrs. Beaghley set out a tray of fruit tarts and a platter with more kinds of doughnuts than I ever knew existed.

Beagle pulled the doughnuts toward him, wrapped his arms around the plate, and started to eat.

"Charles," his mother gasped, nodding toward the dozen or so people at our table, "there are others!"

"I know, Mom," Beagle said, glancing up to look at the fruit tarts. "I'll get to them later."

Pet Confusion   ◨ **2** ◨

As far as I'm concerned, the worst part of school is the bus ride.

The trouble with riding our bus is the eighth-graders. (They were just as bad last year when they were seventh-graders.) Four or five of them like to tease little kids, the littler the better. Since our bus also picks up some of the kids from Somerset Elementary, that means the littlest kids on our bus are first-graders. If the little kids bring food onto the bus, the eighth-graders find it and take it. They eat the cookies, play catch with the apples, and throw the popcorn out the windows.

Our bus driver doesn't care what goes on as long as it doesn't interfere with his driving. Of course, if you complain, he'll give the other kid a pink form to take home to his parents. But even first-graders know that getting somebody else in trouble only makes things worse for you.

Anything can happen on the bus. One day during the first week of school, we got off at our stop and I saw someone had stuck a piece of paper to Beagle's back. At first we thought it was going to be one of those "Kick me" jokes like people play on April Fool's. But this paper was folded over. Beagle opened it, and we saw a drawing of a heart with a knife in it. Below the picture someone had written, "This is for you, creep."

Nothing special happened the next day and life seemed normal, so we didn't talk about the note anymore.

One day Charlie was standing in the aisle of the bus talking to me while the bus was loading outside the school.

"You got a runny nose?" I heard someone saying. I looked around and saw Mac Cartwright, one of the eighth-graders, talking to a second-grader named Ricky.

"You know, kid," Mac was saying, "if your nose

runs and your feet smell, it means you're built upside down. Hey, Ken, wanta check this kid's feet?"

Beagle doesn't stop to think before he acts. He usually does or says the first thing that comes into his head. Sometimes that's the worst thing about him, and then sometimes it's the best thing.

I was just realizing that Ricky was going to be the butt of the jokes for the day when I also realized that Beagle was leaving. He stepped onto the seat beside me, went over the back of the seat, and dropped down between Ricky and Mac.

"So how's it going, Ricky, ol' pal? I gotta finish telling you about the skunk I caught in Taylor's Woods."

Beagle was off and running, talking the ears off a bewildered Ricky.

Mac shrugged and moved on. Dotty Patrick slid into the seat beside me, complaining about her math assignment, and the bus pulled away from the school.

After a few stops things were quieting down as the bus began to empty. In a lull, I overheard Beagle, who still hadn't stopped talking to Ricky, saying, "Do you know how Seattle got its name?"

"Huh-uh," Ricky said.

"Well, you see, there were these two explorers who

21

reached the Pacific Ocean just at the place where Seattle is. And they found a tribe of Indians living there. The Indians were friendly and their chief invited the explorers to come and eat supper with them. The explorers said, 'Sure, we'd love to, but where can we get cleaned up?'

"And the Indian chief raised his arm, waved it toward the Pacific Ocean, and said, 'See, 'at'll wash.'

"And that's how it got to be called Seattle, Wash."

Beagle poked him in the ribs and Ricky giggled. I looked at Dotty, and we both groaned.

By the time Beagle and I get off the bus each day, almost everybody is gone. Ricky, as well as the louder eighth-graders, had been dropped off before we reached our corner. I was about to wave good-bye and head on home when Beagle stopped me.

"I need your help. We have a mystery to solve."

"You know, the real mystery is how you keep finding mysteries."

"This one is something Ricky asked us to help with. I was telling him about our detective agency."

I wondered how Ricky had managed to ask anything at the rate Beagle had been talking to him, but I gave up the idea of going straight home and went with Beagle over to our agency.

"Here's the problem," Beagle said when we were settled at the desk. "A woman in Ricky's neighborhood has gone to Florida for a month, and Ricky is taking care of her pets—a cat, a dog, a gerbil, and a goldfish. He knows their names are Nick, Harry, Walt, and Mo; but she didn't tell him which is which. Ricky says he can't follow the instructions she left for him until he can match the animals with their names."

"What were the instructions?" I asked.

"Here they are. Ricky had them with him because he thought he might find somebody to help him at school."

Beagle spread out the sheet of paper on the desk and we both read:

> *Put three drops from the brown bottle of vitamins into Harry's water each day. Put two drops from the green bottle of vitamins into the gerbil's water every other day. Nick and the goldfish don't get vitamins.*
>
> *Harry and Walt can be fed in the morning and again at night. The dog and the goldfish should only be fed once a day.*

"This is tougher than it looks," I said when I had read through the instructions.

I drew up a chart that looked like this:

	goldfish	cat	dog	gerbil
NICK				
HARRY				
WALT				
MO				

[Can you solve the puzzle? Match the names to the animals before you read Beagle and Ellen's solution on the next page.]

Solution to "Pet Confusion":

We see from the instructions about vitamins that Harry is not the gerbil or the goldfish. The feeding instructions tell us that Harry is not the dog. So Harry is the cat. Nick cannot be the gerbil or the goldfish according to the vitamin instructions; and, of course, he is not the cat. So, Nick must be the dog. Only the gerbil and goldfish are left. Walt, we see from the feeding instructions, is not the goldfish; so he is the gerbil. The goldfish then is Mo.

"There, how did we do?" Beagle asked when the chart was filled.

"That's perfect," I said. "Do you want to give Ricky a call?"

"I think I'll go over to his house instead. I want to give him back his instructions, and I'll explain it to him in person."

The next morning, when Ricky got on the bus, he sat down across the aisle from me, beside another second-grader. After a while I heard him ask his friend, "Wanta know how Seattle got its name?"

His friend must have nodded because Ricky said, "Explorers found the Pacific Ocean and Indians were living there. The Indians said, 'Hey, come and eat with us.' And the explorers said, 'Where can we wash our hands?' And the Indians pointed to the ocean and said, 'See, 'at'll do!'"

The Big
Pig Problem

Near the end of September, Beagle and I took our crayfish back to Turtle Creek. I guess they'll miss the bits of baked chicken, but we figured they'd be happier in the creek. We kept walking along Turtle Creek until we came to the McElroys' farm. I know them, so I was glad to stop in and say hello. And Beagle treats everybody like he has known them all his life even if he has just been introduced.

I went into the kitchen for a drink of water and a chat with Mrs. McElroy, and Beagle stood around outside talking to Mr. McElroy.

"Do you think your friend would like a piece of my blueberry pie?" Mrs. McElroy asked.

I didn't need to check with Beagle. When the question is food, his answer is always yes.

I went out to invite Beagle in and was just in time to hear Mr. McElroy saying, "They're cussed little devils, smart but cussed."

"Here's something you ought to hear, Ellen," Beagle said. "Mr. McElroy is having trouble with his pigs."

"It's those three sows," Mr. McElroy said, "Pearl, Lulu, and Rosy. You never saw their equal for rooting up vegetables."

"But they're penned up," I said. "How can they get your vegetables? Unless they're smart enough to open the pen."

"No, they haven't gotten that far yet." Mr. McElroy laughed. "But they are smart enough to get through the fence I put up to keep rabbits out of my vegetables."

"If they aren't opening the pen, how are they getting out?"

"That's what he's trying to tell you if you'll be quiet, Ellen," Beagle said.

"There are some teenagers from the development on that side of the farm who cut through my land to get home from school, and one of them makes a habit of passing by this pen and opening the gate," Mr. McElroy explained.

28

"Do you know who these kids are?" Beagle asked. "I'll go tell them to lay off."

"Now wait a minute, young Charles. A farmer can't afford hard feelings toward his neighbors. We know which kids walk through our land, but what I would really like to know is which one is the mischief maker."

By now Mrs. McElroy had joined us, and she said, "Ellen, your mother tells me you're pretty good at this kind of thing. Maybe you'd look into it for us."

"I could try, Mrs. McElroy. But I'm not sure what you want me to do."

"We need to know which of the young people is opening that pen every day, and then we'll know how to handle it from there."

"The kids who use the farm for a shortcut are Adam Webb, Gail Carter, Tony Riley, and—who is that other girl?" Mr. McElroy turned to his wife for help.

"That's the Henson girl, Sheila."

"One of those four opens this pen, and I can't catch them at it. He or she always seems to know when I'm watching," Mr. McElroy said.

They told us that the pen had been opened on each of the two previous afternoons, and Beagle suggested they tell us everything they could remember about those two incidents.

"What I remember best is that Rosy almost finished my turnips!" Mrs. McElroy said.

"The first of the kids every day always walks past whistling 'Yankee Doodle,'" Mr. McElroy said.

"Is that a boy or a girl?" Beagle asked.

"It's a funny thing, but when all you've got to go on is a whistle there's no way of telling," Mrs. McElroy said.

"Anyway, the whistler is not the troublemaker," Mr. McElroy added. "The whistler crosses through the cornfield. That's on the far side of the barn from the pig pen."

"Come in, and let's have that blueberry pie," Mrs. McElroy suggested. "After you've eaten, you can decide whether you want to find our culprit for us."

Beagle, of course, thought her suggestion was a great idea. He ate two slices with real farm cream poured over them and told Mrs. McElroy it was the best pie he had ever eaten. I didn't spoil the compliment by telling her that whatever he is eating at the moment is the best ever.

As we left the farm, we promised the McElroys that we would investigate their problem.

"Beagle, these are high school students," I pointed out as soon as we were out of earshot. "How are we going to find out about them?"

"I have ways," Beagle said, which usually means that he knows someone who knows someone who might know something about it.

The only thing I could do was go home and wait to see what he found out.

Beagle, as I learned the next day, knows Sheila Henson's younger brother. Through what he described as "skillful questioning," Beagle had discovered some things about the high school students who cross the McElroys' farm.

1. Sheila, who doesn't know how to whistle, has mentioned at home that someone is turning the McElroys' pigs loose.
2. Sheila and Gail are both afraid of the culprit, who is known for having a temper.
3. Tony, Gail, and the whistler transferred to Fairview last year.

Below Beagle's notes, I made a chart to record the information:

	culprit	whistler
ADAM		
GAIL		
TONY		
SHEILA		

"Beagle," I shouted, "we've done it again. Let's go tell the McElroys who's opening their pig pen."

[Can you identify the culprit? Remember that the whistler is innocent.]

Solution to "The Big Pig Problem":

Sheila can't be the whistler since she doesn't know how to whistle. Since she is afraid of the culprit, she is not the one opening the pen. Clue #2 also eliminates Gail as the culprit, and clue #3 means Gail is not the whistler. Since Tony is not the whistler (clue #3), that means the whistler must be Adam, who is then eliminated as the culprit.

The person who turns the McElroys' pigs loose each day is, therefore, Tony Riley.

The McElroys rewarded us with fresh-baked blackberry cobbler, which Beagle decided was slightly better than blueberry pie and definitely the best reward we'd ever had.

When we left the McElroys' farm, we walked back along the creek and decided to stop in at our agency. Even from a distance we could see that a paper had been stuck onto the door of the shed.

"Maybe it's another case," Beagle said, speeding up.

When I got to the door, he was standing with the paper in his hand, looking puzzled.

"What is it?"

He handed it over without a word, and I read, "You are in big trouble, creep. When you least expect it, I'll get you."

It looked just like the note from the bus, and I had the chilly feeling that this was one puzzle we wouldn't solve easily.

The Mixed-Up Science Experiments ▣ 4 ▣

"Do you need me to explain this problem one more time?" Mr. Shelby asked our seventh grade math class.

"Yes," we all chorused.

"All right. Now, everyone watch the board, and I'll run through it once again."

Beagle raised his hand.

"What is it, Charles?" Mr. Shelby asked wearily.

"Don't you think I should go tell the class next door that you'll be coming through?"

The picture of Mr. Shelby charging through the wall like Superman, scattering chalk dust and bricks, was too much. And I could just imagine the looks on the faces of the class in the next room. Everybody laughed—except, of course, Mr. Shelby.

"You know, Charles, there are two kinds of people in the world," Mr. Shelby said sadly, "problem makers and problem solvers. I'm very much afraid that you're one of the world's problem makers."

Not everybody appreciates Charlie's sense of humor. Our sixth grade teacher certainly didn't, and it looks like Mr. Shelby doesn't either.

By the time school was out, I had almost forgotten about Mr. Shelby running through the wall. I was just walking out of the building when Beagle caught up with me.

"What's up, Beagle?" I asked.

A lot of people think Beagle is just a clown. As a matter of fact, for a long time I thought he was a pain in the neck. He's greedy and selfish. But he can be a good person to know if you need a friend, and he thinks I'm terrific, which makes it pretty hard for me to dislike him.

"Mr. Shelby has a problem," Beagle explained. "If you'll help him, you'll be helping me too."

"He asked *you* for help?"

"No, he didn't even notice me, but this is our big chance. You know how he's always talking about problem solvers and problem makers. He thinks I'm a problem maker. If you help me help him, maybe it would change my image."

36

I wasn't sure of Beagle's reasoning, but I can't pass up a chance to solve a mystery.

Instead of going back to our own homeroom, Beagle took me to the eighth grade science class, where we found Mr. Shelby standing beside a large table at the back of the room. On the table were four science exhibits, the first- through fourth-place winners in the eighth grade science fair.

"What's wrong, Mr. Shelby?" I asked.

"Someone has removed the ribbons from these exhibits and I don't know which one gets which award."

"Can't you just wait until tomorrow and ask the students?"

"Unfortunately, I have less than an hour to deliver these to the fairgrounds for the statewide science fair exhibit," Mr. Shelby answered. He went on to explain that the teacher who headed the science program was away at a conference and had asked him to see that the exhibits were delivered on time.

Beagle was studying the exhibits, which included an electrical current experiment, a study of the effects of chocolate on rats, an acid rain experiment, and a comparison of the effects of different amounts of light on bean sprouts.

"Give us a few minutes," Beagle said. "Let me and

Ellen see what we can find out from people who are still in the building."

Mr. Shelby didn't say yes but he didn't exactly disagree either. I took a moment to copy down the names of the people whose projects had won prizes. They were Betty Lewis, Richard Walker, Daniel Mann, and Joanne Morse. Then Beagle and I set off to look for eighth-graders.

"There's Terry Hale!" Beagle cried. "Catch her, and I'll take a look upstairs."

Terry, I soon discovered, didn't remember anything about the science projects except that her algae grown in a fish bowl hadn't won a prize.

Then, I spotted John Farrar coming out of the auditorium and dashed off to talk to him.

John turned out to be a friend of Daniel Mann, whose exhibit had won a prize.

"I'm not sure which ribbon he got," John said, "but it wasn't first or second place because I remember telling him that he should have gotten one or the other of those."

While we were talking, another eighth-grader joined us and said he remembered that Betty Lewis had said that she and the first- and third-place winners had worked on their projects together.

38

They wished me luck and left while I was writing down what they had told me. I had just finished when Beagle found me.

"I found a couple of people upstairs, but I didn't learn much," he said. "Someone remembered that Joanne Morse complained that the first-place winner used an idea that she suggested. And, Daniel Mann was overheard saying that the third-place winner is a friend of his, but he was very critical of the second-place winner. Not much, is it?"

"I think it's enough. Let's go talk to Mr. Shelby," I suggested.

We found him in our seventh-grade room looking sadder than ever.

"Just a minute, Mr. Shelby. I think we can help you," Beagle said.

Beagle added his clues to mine and together we studied the list, which now looked like this:

1. John thought Daniel should have received the first- or second-place ribbon instead of the one he did get.
2. Betty and the first- and third-place winners worked together.
3. Joanne said the first-place winner used an idea that she had thought of first.

4. Daniel is a friend of the third-place winner but was critical of the second-place winner.

That was all we had been able to find out, but I was sure it would be enough. So I drew up a grid that looked like this:

	first	second	third	fourth
BETTY				
RICHARD				
DANIEL				
JOANNE				

Beagle and I worked together, scratching in x's and o's.

"Here, Mr. Shelby," I said in a few minutes. "If you take a look at this, I think you'll see which ribbon belongs to which person."

[Can you sort out the science projects? Find your own solution and then check your answer against Ellen and Beagle's on the next page.]

Solution to "The Mixed-Up Science Experiments":

Daniel did not win first or second place (clue #1). He also did not win third place (clue #4). So, he must be the fourth-place winner.

Clue #2 indicates that Betty did not win first or third place, and we know she cannot be the fourth-place winner since that is Daniel. So Betty won second place.

According to clue #3, Joanne did not win first place. Since we have identified the second- and fourth-place winners, Joanne must have won the third-place ribbon.

Of course, that means that Richard won first place.

"Thanks, Ellen," Beagle said, after we had helped Mr. Shelby put the ribbons on the exhibits and load them into his car. "Mr. Shelby was actually smiling at me before he left."

"I was glad to help, Beagle. But do you realize that now we have another problem?"

"What's that?"

"We've missed the bus."

More Trouble
for Beagle

Almost three weeks passed and nothing happened to Beagle after he got that threatening note. We talked about it with other people in our class and everybody agreed that it must have been one of the eighth-graders' not-so-funny jokes.

Then one day I walked into Mr. Shelby's room after lunch to find ten or twelve people crowding in front of the blackboard.

Beagle stepped back from the group and said, "Go take a look."

So I peeked over someone's shoulder. All across the chalkboard, written in spray paint, were the words: MR. SHELBY STINKS. Below the paint was the picture of the head of a little dog, like this:

There was no doubt about it: The dog was meant to be a beagle, and it looked just like the little drawings Charlie puts under his name on all his schoolwork.

I've thought a lot of bad things about Beagle, and most of them were right. Once he even had the idea of taking people's dogs and then collecting a reward for "finding" them. But not for one second did I think he had painted those words on the board. I didn't know who wrote that message, but I realized I might be the only person who was sure it wasn't Beagle.

"Who?" I asked.

"I dunno." Beagle was really puzzled. He'd never had a real enemy in his life, at least not until now.

"What are we going to do?" I asked.

Beagle grinned. "Thanks for saying it in the plural. I guess I could use some help. The only thing I can think of is to try to convince Mr. Shelby that I'd never do this."

Mr. Shelby had been almost friendly since Beagle and I had helped him sort out the science exhibits. But if he thought Beagle did this, that would be the end of the friendship.

School was almost over for the day before I had another chance to speak to Beagle.

"I've talked to Mr. Shelby and the principal," he said. "Mr. Shelby says he's willing to withhold judgment until there's more evidence. The principal said that if I wanted to clear myself, I could try to find out where the spray paint came from."

"Well, how do we do that?"

"You mean you're willing to help?"

"We're partners, aren't we?"

"Thanks, Ellen. If you're ever in trouble, I'll help you out."

He had practically saved my life on one of our cases last summer, but I didn't remind him.

The trouble with finding the owner of the spray paint was that the paint used on the chalkboard was a special metallic blue that had also been used for two graffiti designs on the outside wall of the school and the sidewalk by the gym. Nobody wanted to admit to owning that paint.

After three days we narrowed the list of suspects to a small gang of eighth-graders that called themselves the

Ghouls. Their names were Ross, Donald, Glen, and Vance. So we concentrated on finding out everything we could about their gang.

Nobody was more surprised than I was to find out that the rest of the seventh-graders also thought Beagle was innocent. I guess they understood his sense of humor better than I had thought.

My friend Dotty and a couple of the guys who hang around with Beagle helped us ask questions. Everybody knew something about the Ghouls, but nobody knew who the leader was. The gang had kept his identity a secret.

By the end of the week, we had learned:

1. Glen was a new member of the group. Vance had brought him into the gang in September, and the Ghouls' leader had agreed to let him in.
2. Donald and the gang's leader had talked the owner of the spray paint into using it on the sidewalk by the gym.
3. Vance and the owner of the spray paint had sprayed the wall of the school with the leader's permission.

"Can we tell who owns the spray paint?" Beagle asked when it began to look as though we had learned everything we possibly could.

"I think so," I said. "Let's try it and see."

I drew a chart like this:

	Ghouls' leader	owner of spray paint
ROSS		
DONALD		
GLEN		
VANCE		

And Beagle and I began to study the clues.

[Do you know which suspect owns the spray paint? You will need to identify the leader first. When you have studied the clues and found your own answer, check it against Beagle and Ellen's solution on the next page.]

Solution to "More Trouble for Beagle":

From the first clue we learn that neither Glen nor Vance is the leader, and the second clue tells us that Donald is not the leader. The leader, therefore, is Ross. Since he is the leader, Ross does not own the spray paint and neither does Donald (clue #2). Vance is not the owner, according to clue #3. So the owner of the spray paint must be Glen.

Confronted with what we had found out, Glen admitted to owning the paint. He also admitted that he was responsible for the graffiti outside the school.

"So why are you still looking depressed?" I asked Beagle.

"Glen says someone took his last can of spray paint more than a week ago. He admits the graffiti, but he says he didn't spray the words on Mr. Shelby's board. The trouble is—I believe him."

"But it could have been him," I argued. I wanted the mystery solved.

Beagle explained that he believed the same person who tried to get him in trouble by spraying Mr. Shelby's board had also written the two threatening notes.

"Why couldn't that be Glen?" I asked.

"Two reasons," Beagle said. "Before this happened, I didn't even know Glen. And, one of those notes was given to me on the bus. Glen doesn't ride the bus."

I groaned. If Beagle was right, something worse might be in store for him.

Grandma Beaghley's
Secret Recipe   ◘ 6 ◘

Beagle didn't get punished for the paint on Mr. Shelby's chalkboard. Nobody could prove he was guilty. But nobody was sure he wasn't.

"I don't know," Beagle said, shaking his head. "No matter what I do Mr. Shelby still doesn't seem to like me. I can't figure out what I'm doing wrong."

"Maybe you could try being quiet for a few days," I suggested, but Beagle's mind was already on something else.

"I signed us up to help with the Halloween carnival, because Mr. Shelby is the faculty sponsor, and I thought maybe that would impress him."

"Us?"

"Yeah, I knew you wouldn't want to be left out."

"No, I guess not." I didn't point out that I could

49

have signed up for myself if I had wanted to. "What did I volunteer to do?"

"Well, you have two jobs so far. You have to bake three dozen cookies, and you'll work at the refreshment stand."

An awful suspicion occurred to me. "Beagle," I asked, "what are *you* going to do?"

"I'm bringing food, too, and I'll work with you at the refreshment stand."

That was what I'd been afraid of. "I hope you don't eat up all the school's profit."

On Saturday morning, Beagle stopped by my house to say he needed help getting ready for the carnival.

"I want to bring peanut butter meatballs. You serve them on toothpicks, and they taste terrific. I thought it was a great idea."

"So what's the problem?"

"It's my grandmother's recipe, and she won't give it to me."

"You can always make something else."

"I guess so, but I really wanted to make the meatballs. Would you go talk to my grandmother with me?"

"Aw, Beagle, I don't know."

Beagle is always talking me into some dumb thing.

If his grandmother wanted to keep her recipe, I thought she was entitled to. On the other hand, if Beagle couldn't talk her into giving up a recipe, she sounded like the kind of person I wanted to meet.

So, as soon as Beagle said "please," I said "okay," and we were on our way.

"It's my own recipe," Grandma Beaghley said when Beagle explained that he wanted to make meatballs for the Halloween carnival, "and I'm very careful about who I give it to."

"But I'm your grandson!" Beagle yelped. "You make it sound like I'm some stranger who walked in and asked for your recipe."

"That's exactly what I mean," she said, nodding just as though this remark explained everything.

And then I had an inspiration.

"I wonder if we could earn the recipe. Are there any chores we could do for you, Mrs. Beaghley?" I asked.

It had occurred to me that maybe she didn't mind giving Beagle the recipe but wanted something in return.

A gleam came into her eye, and I knew I was right.

"Now, let me see," she said thoughtfully. "Maybe I have just the thing."

Grandma Beaghley left the room and came back with a stack of old papers.

She explained that she was the secretary of the local historical society and that the papers had come to the society as part of a bequest that included the Kimble Mansion. The house had been built on the riverfront in 1749 and had played a key role in the city's history. In the late 1800s it was an inn. After that, it was used as a school until the 1950s.

"As soon as restoration is completed, we're going to open the building to the public. I'm trying to write up a history of the house, which we'll print as a brochure. And here's my problem," she said.

She told us she wanted to know what had happened to the children of Peter Landrum Kimble, the man who built the house. From the few available sources of information, she had learned that the children's names were Mathilda, Joel, Nathan, William, and Helen. She knew that one of Kimble's children returned to England as an adult, one became a storekeeper, and one fought in the Revolution. Those were the only facts known for sure. Now, Mrs. Beaghley wanted to discover which Kimble had done each of those things.

As Beagle and I settled down to read through the old papers she gave us, Grandma Beaghley brought us crackers with cream cheese and a plateful of peanut butter meatballs.

After a couple of hours of reading through musty old papers, I asked Beagle if he thought it was really worth it.

He said, "Maybe."

So I ate another meatball and kept reading.

When we finally wrote down all the information we had found, it looked like this:

1. The Kimble who had moved to England wrote to Mathilda after their brother was killed in the Revolution.
2. Nathan was godfather to one of the store-keeper's children.
3. William visited the English Kimble in 1785.
4. Nathan, who did not fight in the Revolution, remained in America throughout his life.
5. Helen and William outlived both the store-keeper and the soldier.

"I don't think we'll ever sort this out," Beagle said.

"At least we can make up a chart and give it a try."

I drew a chart like this:

	storekeeper	moved to England	fought in war
MATHILDA			
JOEL			
NATHAN			
WILLIAM			
HELEN			

"I give up," Beagle said. "I can see what some of them *weren't,* but I don't see what any of them *were.*"

"That's the whole point. If we can just eliminate enough people in any one category, we'll be able to match a person with that category just because he or she is the only one left. Anyway, let's try it and see how much we can find out."

[Beagle thinks this puzzle can't be solved, but Ellen thinks it can. Of course she's right. See if you can find the answer before you read her solution on the next page.]

Solution to "Grandma Beaghley's Secret Recipe":

Mathilda can be eliminated as the person who moved to England and as the one who fought in the Revolution (clue #1). Clue #2 eliminates Nathan as the storekeeper. Clue #3 means that William is not the one who moved to England. Clue #4 eliminates Nathan as the one who moved to England and as the one who fought in the war. Both Helen and William can be eliminated as the storekeeper and as the one who fought in the war (clue #5). At this point your chart should look like this:

	storekeeper	moved to England	fought in war
MATHILDA		X	X
JOEL			
NATHAN	X	X	X
WILLIAM	X	X	X
HELEN	X		X

It now becomes obvious that Joel is the only one who could have fought in the Revolutionary War. So, we put an o beside his name under that category and cross him out of the other two categories. And then it is evident that Mathilda owned the store, and Helen is the one who moved to England.

As we left Grandma Beaghley's, Beagle was studying her recipe:

Peanut Butter Meatballs

½ cup peanut butter
½ pound ground beef
¼ cup chopped onion (or 1 tablespoon instant, minced onion)
2 tablespoons chili sauce
1 teaspoon salt
⅛ teaspoon pepper
¼ cup flour

Preheat oven to 400°. In a large bowl, mix the peanut butter, beef, onion, chili sauce, salt, and pepper. Shape into 30 small meatballs, about one inch across. Put the flour on a plate and roll the meatballs lightly in the flour to coat them on all sides. Put on ungreased baking sheet and bake for 12–15 minutes. Drain on paper towels.

"I knew there'd be beef and peanut butter," Beagle said.

"I think I could have guessed the onion," I added, "but I never suspected the chili sauce. You know, Beagle, you got what you wanted. You should look happier."

"I was just thinking," he said. "It doesn't make sense that we can find out so much about people who lived two hundred years ago and we can't find out who painted Mr. Shelby's board two weeks ago."

Which Witch? ◻ 7 ◻

The Halloween carnival was held in the school's gymnasium on the next Friday. For the school, it was a huge success. For Beagle, although we didn't know it then, it was the beginning of the end.

Under Mr. Shelby's direction, everybody had worked hard on the fun house, the booths, the activities. Beagle, who turned out to be a great salesman, made a big success of the refreshment stand. I made six dozen cookies instead of the three dozen I was signed up for, just in case Beagle wanted to eat some. He made a point, however, of paying for anything he ate, and that cut down his appetite.

When we finished our turn working at the refreshment stand, I rushed off to have a chance at some of the games—apple bobbing, ring toss, and guessing the number of jelly beans in a fish bowl.

I had just come out of the haunted house when Beagle came running up.

"Richard Higley wants to hire us to solve a problem for him."

Since Richard is one of the nice eighth-graders, helping him was okay with me.

"What's his problem?" I asked.

Richard had just had his fortune told at a little booth run by the eighth-graders, where the fortune-tellers were dressed as witches instead of gypsies.

To his surprise, Richard hadn't heard a prediction at all. Disguised by her witch's costume, the eighth grade girl had told him that she liked him. And now Richard wanted to know who she was.

"What do you say? Do we take the case?"

This one was tricky. Richard wanted to know who the girl was, but did the girl want Richard to know?

"Okay, if we agree on one thing," I told Charlie. "When we find the girl, if she doesn't want us to tell Richard who she is, we won't tell."

Beagle agreed, and we set out to find out all we could about the fortune-telling booth.

The eighth grade girls who had been taking turns

playing the fortune-teller were Julia, Kim, Linda, and Ruth.

Because the predictions were supposed to be mysterious, none of the girls were willing to admit whose fortunes they had told. All the secrecy made it hard to find out anything, but Richard had told us that his fortune-teller had worn a purple hat. At least that was a starting point.

A quick check told us that all the witches were dressed in black; one of them was wearing a purple hat and another one a red wig. Though all the girls refused to say who was who, they didn't seem to mind talking to us. Just as we were running out of things to say, I nodded to Beagle. I thought we had enough clues to figure out which one had told Richard's fortune.

Our final list of clues looked like this:

1. The girl in the purple hat had taken her turn in the booth before Ruth and the girl in the red wig.
2. Both Linda and the girl in the red wig noticed that Richard was standing in line to have his fortune told.
3. The girl in the red wig had suggested that the girl in the purple hat trade turns with Kim to be able to tell Richard's fortune.

On a borrowed sheet of paper, I drew up a chart so that Beagle and I could check off the information:

	purple hat	red wig
JULIA		
KIM		
LINDA		
RUTH		

[Richard wants to know who wore the purple hat. Remember that the girl in the purple hat did not wear the red wig. Can you identify her before you read Ellen and Beagle's solution?]

Solution to "Which Witch?":

Clue #1 eliminates Ruth as both the girl in the purple hat and the one in the red wig. Linda did not wear the red wig (clue #2). Kim did not wear the purple hat or the red wig (clue #3). At this point we know that Julia is the only one who could have worn the red wig. Julia, therefore, can't be the girl in the purple hat. So Linda wore the purple hat and told Richard that she secretly likes him.

As soon as we told Linda that we had discovered her secret, she admitted it.

"I know he likes me too and being disguised gave me the courage to tell him that I like him. Sure, you can go ahead and tell him who I am."

"We just traded being Sherlock Holmes for playing Cupid. Yuck!" Beagle said.

As the carnival ended, Mr. Shelby called his helpers together to tell us what a terrific job he thought we had done. The carnival was such a success that it set a new record with the money we raised for the school. The night ended on a note of triumph that had most of us pitching in to help the cleanup crew.

While we waited for my mom to pick both of us up, Beagle and I watched a vampire, several monsters, and a whole string of rock stars drift past us into the night. After a while, we were all alone.

"Everybody else is gone. What's keeping my mom?" I asked and shivered, only partly from the chill in the air.

For no real reason I could have explained, I suddenly felt scared.

I had just leaned forward once again to look for Mom's car when a figure in a long cape leaped in front of us. In spite of being startled, I realized it was just someone from the carnival wearing one of those rubbery monster masks that you pull on over your whole head.

"Hey, trick or treat," Beagle greeted him.

"It won't be any treat for you," the monster growled in a low voice. "You're finished at this school, and by tomorrow you'll know it."

I made a quick grab for the black cape, but the figure sidestepped me and set off at a run. Beagle tried a flying tackle and missed.

We had lost out on our first real chance to find out who was behind Beagle's troubles.

Mom tooted the horn as Beagle picked himself up. We hadn't seen her drive up.

"What was that all about?" she asked as we climbed into the car.

I thought it was about time we told the whole story to somebody, but, while I was deciding where to begin, Beagle answered.

"Nothing, Mrs. Sloan. It was just a Halloween prank."

I whispered, "Tell her."

Charlie shook his head and glared at me.

It wasn't my secret to tell, but I couldn't help wishing he would tell somebody. The trouble was more than just eighth-graders playing tricks on us seventh-graders. Somebody was out to get Beagle.

A Thief for
Captain Holloway   ◼ 8 ◼

_____

On Saturday morning after the Halloween carnival, I was still sleeping when the phone rang. I knew it was going to be Beagle. Who else would call at dawn on the morning after a party?

But as soon as he had explained why he had called, I was wide awake and no longer annoyed. The night before, a crime had been committed at Goose Valley Mall, and Sara Cottle, who owned Cottle's Curio Shop, wanted to hire Beagle and me to help solve it.

"She said Captain Holloway is in charge of the case, so I called him to ask if he minded if you and I investigated. He's still thanking us for our help in the Lockridge diamond robbery. He said he'd be glad to have our help again."

I dressed and ate breakfast in record-breaking time. When Beagle's mother drove up, Beagle jumped out and ran toward my door, but I was out to meet him before he could ring the bell.

"Come on," he cried. "I'll explain in the car."

I glanced at Charlie as we drove off. I couldn't forget the threatening figure that had jumped at us out of the darkness at school last night, but Beagle was obviously thinking only of the mystery at the mall.

"What's all this about?" I asked, opening up the notebook that I had remembered to bring along.

"A troupe of players has been performing four shows on Fridays and Saturdays for the past two week-ends. The merchants sponsored the shows, so they're free to the audiences. Last night jewels from a traveling display on view at the mall were stolen. The jewels disappeared between closing time last night and six this morning. Everybody who had access to the mall during that time has been cleared except the members of this performing group."

"Was Mrs. Cottle's shop robbed too?"

"No, it's more complicated than that. She wasn't robbed, but her niece is one of the performers who are suspected."

Suddenly I was remembering the last time Beagle

66

and I had tried to catch a thief and had ended up facing a crook with a gun. I gulped.

"Captain Holloway told me all he has learned about the troupe. It seems pretty clear one of them has to be the thief," Beagle was saying. "He also told me one of the group used to be a magician. The troupe was formed by this magician and another guy named Tony."

Most of the stores weren't open when we got to the mall, but Beagle had said Mrs. Cottle was planning to meet us at her shop. We saw her as soon as we got off the escalator on the second level.

"I'm so glad you're willing to help," she said. "Come inside and let's talk."

"One thing I don't know yet," I said when we were settled in the back of her shop, "is the names of the performers."

"Here they are," Mrs. Cottle said, handing me a green flyer advertising the performances in the mall.

As Mrs. Cottle began to talk, I copied down the names: Fred Buckles, Denise Hammaker, Phillip King, Lynn Dorman, and Tony Burley.

"Last night was their last performance," Mrs. Cottle told us. "After the show the group moved on to Phila-delphia where they're scheduled to give a matinée today. I suppose the police will have the whole group picked up, but they would like to know as much as possible before they do. And I would like to know the truth before my niece is picked up as a suspect.

"You see, Denise is my sister's daughter, and I'm the one who recommended that the merchants hire this group. I want to protect my niece, but the thief must be found. I feel responsible."

"Do you think your niece was involved in the theft?" Beagle asked.

Mrs. Cottle hesitated.

"I'm almost sure she wasn't, but she has been so apologetic these last two days that looking back I suspect she knew the theft was planned. And, also, Pinewood Shopping Center was burglarized when her troupe was there in the summer. I think she suspected one of her fellow players."

"We'll have to tell Captain Holloway everything we find out," I explained.

"Yes, of course. The one thing I didn't feel I could turn over to the police was Denise's journal. It was pure accident that she left it behind at all. I don't want to turn it over as evidence, but, if she knew something of the thief's plans, the police must be told."

Mrs. Cottle gave us the journal and went out to open her shop since it was now ten o'clock. The journal was really a datebook that listed appointments with a whole page for each week. Occasionally Denise had written a comment beside a date. Beagle and I decided to concentrate on the months of September and October.

"While you read, I'm going to go over to the coffee shop for a couple of Danish pastries. I don't know about you, but I didn't have much time for breakfast," Beagle said.

By the time Beagle got back I had added a few more notes to the list I had started in the car. My complete list of clues looked like this:

1. One of the performers was originally a magician.
2. Tony and the magician formed the acting group five years ago.
3. On October 20, Lynn and the magician told the rest of the group that they were going to be married.
4. Fred told Denise not to tell this to the magician, but the thief is angry because he thought Lynn would marry him.

"Why don't you know who the magician is?" Beagle asked, passing me a lemon Danish and a carton of milk.

"Because Denise uses a kind of shorthand when she makes notes in her journal. See," I said, pointing to one entry. "She draws a top hat instead of writing out the magician's name. For the thief she uses a bandit's mask."

"Not very original," Beagle said, and I knew he was thinking of the drawing of a dog that had been used to incriminate him.

"I think we may have enough information to tell who in the group is the thief," I said to change the subject.

"Captain Holloway didn't expect us to find the thief," Beagle said, cheering up. "All he was hoping for was that we would eliminate a suspect or two."

"Well, let's give it a try," I said, drawing a chart so we could check off the information we had found:

	thief	magician
FRED		
DENISE		
PHILLIP		
LYNN		
TONY		

[Can you find the thief? The thief and the magician are not the same person, but you will need to find the magician in order to identify the thief. When you think you know the answer, turn the page and check it against Beagle and Ellen's solution.]

Solution to "A Thief for Captain Holloway":

The fourth clue is the most important. From it we learn that the thief is one of the men, but he is not Fred or the magician. The magician is also a man as we know from clue #3. The magician isn't Tony (clue #2) or Fred (clue #4). So the magician is Phillip. Since the magician is not the thief, we can now eliminate Phillip. And that means Tony is the thief.

"Thanks to the two of you, we've caught another thief," Captain Holloway said as we relaxed in his office after he had made arrangements to have Tony Burley picked up in Philadelphia.

Just then the phone on the captain's desk rang.

Most of his end of the conversation consisted of a series of *hmmms*. Finally he said, "Yes, Mike, he is here. You were right to let me know."

He put the phone back, and I think we both knew trouble was coming. For a moment no one spoke.

"Ellen," Captain Holloway began, "Charlie, you two have been a big help to the police, and I'm grateful."

I looked sideways at Beagle, but he was concentrating very hard on Captain Holloway.

"That call was from my desk sergeant, reporting to me on a call from your principal. Last night somebody vandalized the school." The captain was speaking very slowly and distinctly. I had the feeling he didn't like what he had to say.

"Three windows were broken in the library. A big metal tub, the one used to bob for apples at your carnival, was set on the library floor, filled with books, and then filled with water."

"That's awful," I said as Captain Holloway paused again, and the silence seemed to stretch out. Beagle wasn't saying a word. "Do they know who did it?"

"Your principal thinks he knows. He says this is the second instance where someone—apparently the same person—has left a kind of signature, a sort of catch-me-if-you-can challenge."

Beagle still wasn't talking, and my heart had dropped down to my feet.

"What sort of signature?" I asked.

"A cartoon drawing of a dog, a beagle."

Grandma Beaghley
Helps Out

We just sat there in Captain Holloway's office feeling stunned after we heard about what had happened at the school.

Finally, we began to talk, starting with the first note and ending with the threat from the masked figure at the carnival. I added that Beagle and I had been together from the time we finished cleaning up after the carnival until my mom had dropped him off at his house. He and I had been alone for a few minutes, but I could vouch for the fact that we hadn't spent the time destroying property.

"I'd like for you two to listen while I call and talk to your principal."

Captain Holloway put through a call to Barnaby

Walters, our principal, and Beagle and I listened as the captain expressed first his concern for what had happened at the school and then his conviction that Charlie Beaghley couldn't be responsible, that it wasn't in his character. And, he went on to explain to Mr. Walters, I had given Beagle an alibi.

When he hung up the phone, Captain Holloway said to us, "My judgment of character isn't perfect, but I'd back you two against any odds."

He had more than repaid us for any help we had given him.

Outside the station, Beagle's mom was waiting for us.

"Mr. Shelby is at our house," she said. "He insists on talking to you, Charles."

"How about coming home with us, Ellen? I think I'm going to need you to give me that alibi one more time," Beagle said.

At Beagle's house, a grim-looking Mr. Shelby sat on the edge of a chair facing an equally grim Grandma Beaghley.

"When there's trouble," Mr. Shelby began, "it's natural to look first to the troublemakers. I had hoped you were going to change this year, Charles. Apparently I was wrong. I have shown the principal some of your papers and explained your habit of drawing a small dog on your schoolwork. While it's possible that someone copied your drawing, Mr. Walters and I think the obvious answer is that you are the culprit. We believe you damaged the school library and then flouted authority by adding that drawing."

Grandma Beaghley sniffed and said, "A farrago!" She told me to sit beside her. Then she sent Beagle's mom to make coffee and told Beagle to bring her a box of historical society materials that she had left on a table in the hall.

"I have a bit of a problem that I want these two to solve for me," she said.

"Mrs. Beaghley," Mr. Shelby said impatiently, "I know Ellen is good at puzzles. I am here because of damage that was done at the school last night."

Ignoring him, Mrs. Beaghley continued, "My problem concerns a series of strange pranks that were played at Hadley High School during the 1950s. Pranksters and vandals are often two very different kinds of people. Don't you agree, Mr. Shelby?" she concluded with sudden fierceness.

For some reason, Mr. Shelby looked pale. "I—I don't think we need to go into ancient history, Mrs. Beaghley."

76

"And I think we do. Some people have very short memories, Mr. Shelby. Charles here may enjoy an ill-timed joke in class, but I think that's poor evidence for his destroying school property. And, if I understand what you've told me, your main reason for believing he's the vandal is the fact that he keeps making people laugh in your classes. Laughing is a real crime," she concluded sarcastically.

"Suppose I simply concede your point," Mr. Shelby offered.

"I wouldn't dream of letting you. I intend to *prove* my point," Grandma said as she accepted the box Beagle held out to her. "Just give me a moment to find what I'm looking for. Ah, here it is, right on top."

Grandma pulled out a thin, yellowed newspaper called *The Hadley High News,* turned a page and folded open the paper to point to a small write-up.

Phantoms Strike Again

Our Phantom Joker has struck again. The latest prank delayed classes for more than an hour as the Phantoms packed snow against the school doors and sprayed it with water to form a wall of ice. Who are these Phantoms?

Well, this reporter has learned that their names are Willis, Bones, Moose, and Tom, but that's all the identification we can give you.

Early last month, Mr. Hodges arrived to find a Volkswagen parked outside the door to the principal's office.

Last week a bottle of food coloring turned all the school's water supply orange.

The leader of the Phantoms is known as the Joker, and he is reportedly the prankster responsible for Hadley High's rash of practical jokes. Who is the Joker? The Phantoms aren't saying.

Willis admits he persuaded the owner of the VW to lend it to the Joker. Bones and the car's owner asked Moose to supply the food coloring. And Moose said the car owner and the Joker refused to tell him where they'll strike next.

"Can you figure out which one of the four Phantoms is the Joker?" Grandma Beaghley asked when we had had a chance to read the newspaper article.

"I think so," I answered. "The three clues in the last paragraph should give it away."

I turned to a clean page in my notebook and made up a chart based on the clues we had:

	owner of VW	joker
MOOSE		
TOM		
WILLIS		
BONES		

"You take this one," I suggested to Beagle and passed my notebook and pencil over to him.

Glancing back and forth from the newspaper to the notebook, he filled in the chart.

"Okay, it's done," he said.

"Now, would you mind explaining it to Mr. Shelby?" Grandma Beaghley asked.

[Using the last paragraph of the newspaper article, see if you can find out which one of the Phantoms of Hadley High was the Joker. Check your answer against Beagle's solution on the next page.]

Solution to "Grandma Beaghley Helps Out":

The first sentence of the last paragraph of the newspaper article tells us that Willis is neither the car owner nor the Joker. From the second sentence we learn that Bones is not the car owner and neither is Moose. The last sentence reveals that Moose is not the Joker. It is now clear that Tom must be the owner of the car, which means Bones is the Joker.

"How's that?" Beagle asked when he finished the explanation.

"A–plus," his grandmother said, just as if we had been in a classroom. "Now, Mr. Shelby, perhaps there's something you'd like to add to this little puzzle."

"I don't believe so. Clever reasoning, Charles."

"Thank you," Beagle replied.

"I think there is something more to say," Mrs. Beaghley insisted, looking at Mr. Shelby over her glasses, which had slipped to the very end of her nose. "Are you trying to say that you know nothing more about this particular news item?"

"I never said that."

"Then I'd like for you to tell these two young people what you do know. Perhaps you've heard of some of the people in this story."

"Since you obviously already know, 'Bones' was my nickname in high school. All of that was just youthful fun."

"Of course. That's my point exactly. You have grown up to be an outstanding teacher. Willis Ford is in the state senate, and your friend 'Moose' is, I believe, president of a law firm. I don't know what became of Tom."

"He's coach of the football team at Monroe County High," Mr. Shelby volunteered.

"A sense of humor doesn't make a person a vandal."

"Quite the opposite, I should think," conceded Mr. Shelby. "I never wanted to think it was you, Charlie, but the evidence . . ."

". . . is wrong," Mrs. Beaghley said firmly. "Now stay and have coffee and cake with us."

The Name Game   ▣ **10** ▣

"**I**f your last name is Paper, you shouldn't name your daughter Tara," Dotty said.

"If your last name is Ho," I said, "you shouldn't name your daughter Ida."

Something went whizzing past our faces.

"What was that?" Dotty asked.

Concentrating on thinking up trick names, the two of us hadn't been paying attention to the other people on the bus as we rode to school.

What had caught our attention was a white object that flew past us toward the front of the bus.

"It's Beagle!" Dotty cried, catching a glimpse through the crowd of kids who were half-standing and peering forward.

"What happened to him?" I asked.

"He got hit by an egg, a raw egg. Ooh, it's all gooey and stuck in his hair."

I quickly turned around and tried looking toward the rear of the bus. The egg had been thrown from behind us, and it had come from over my left shoulder.

The last three seats on the left of the bus were taken by Mac Cartwright and his friends. Mac was sitting beside Ken. Candace and Jenny, two eighth grade girls, were behind them. Patty and Eric were in the last seat, and a guy named Tyrone was standing in the aisle talking to Mac. All seven of them were eighth-graders, and one of them had thrown the egg, but there was no way to tell which one.

I glanced at Mr. Morris, the bus driver, but I knew he wouldn't be any help. He only gets tough with kids who bother him.

Under cover of the confusion, I pulled out my notebook and wrote down the seven names. One of those people, I thought, hates Beagle enough to throw a raw egg at him. On the way home it wouldn't have been so bad, but now Beagle would have to wash off as well as he could and try to get through the day.

As the bus stopped at school, I ran to catch up with Beagle. He had already cleaned away most of the egg.

"We'll get him," I managed to say. "We keep solving problems for other people. It's about time we solved one for ourselves."

And then we were surrounded by people from our class. Everybody was sympathetic. As far as they knew it was just another case of eighth-graders taking it out on us seventh-graders.

With math, science, gym, English, and everything, there's almost never time to spare for your own problems at school. The day was almost over before I had a chance to think about Beagle's secret enemy.

In history, our last class of the day, Mrs. Lightner explained that she had something different for us to do. "This is a name puzzle," she said.

For a moment I thought of the name game Dotty and I had been playing on the bus. But, of course, Mrs. Lightner's puzzle wasn't like our game.

First, Mrs. Lightner gave us the names of five men, all of whom had been explorers, and told us that one of them had discovered a Pacific island and another of them had founded a colony on the island. The men's names were Jasper Camp, Gilbert Arms, Calvin Wayne, Ernest Deavor, and Eugene Branton.

Then she gave us some information about the men:

1. Both the man who discovered the island and the man who founded the first colony were sailors with Gilbert Arms.

2. The island's discoverer and Calvin bought a ship of their own two years before the island was discovered.

3. Eugene and the founder of the colony returned to the mainland after the death of the island's discoverer.

4. The founder of the colony was the uncle of Jasper and the second cousin of the island's discoverer.

And finally, she asked us two questions: Who discovered the island? Who founded the colony?

Everybody groaned. "Who knows?" somebody asked. I almost laughed. It might sound tough to the other kids, but Charlie and I know this sort of puzzle backwards. I turned around to grin at Beagle, but he was already at work. I decided I'd better get started too and began drawing up a chart:

	discoverer of the island	founder of the colony
JASPER		
GILBERT		
CALVIN		
ERNEST		
EUGENE		

I had just figured out the answers to the two questions when Mrs. Lightner called for our attention.

"Class, Charles Beaghley will give us the answers and explain how he worked them out."

For once, Beagle had beaten me to an answer. As far as I was concerned, it couldn't have happened at a better time. This hadn't been Beagle's best semester.

[Can you find the answers to Mrs. Lightner's questions? Try to solve the puzzle before you read Beagle's answer on the next page.]

Solution to "The Name Game":

Clue #1 tells us that Gilbert Arms is neither the discoverer of the island nor the founder of the colony. Clue #3 reveals that Eugene cannot be either of these people. And Jasper is neither the founder of the colony nor the discoverer of the island (clue #4). Calvin is eliminated by clue #2 as the island's discoverer, which means that Ernest discovered the island. Calvin, therefore, is the founder of the colony.

Beagle had just finished explaining the puzzle when the public address system clicked on. We always know when the principal is going to make an announcement because the speaker clicks before the voice comes through.

"Mrs. Lightner," Mr. Walters said, "I believe Charles Beaghley is in your class at this hour. Would you send him to my office immediately?"

The public address system clicked off.

What now? I wondered.

"It's almost the end of the class, Charles. You'd better take all your things with you," Mrs. Lightner said.

Maybe it was my imagination, but I thought she sounded sympathetic.

School ended, and when I headed for the bus, I still didn't know why the principal wanted to see Beagle.

I sat down in the seat that Dotty had saved for me and wondered if Beagle would miss the bus.

The driver was already closing the doors when Beagle showed up. He climbed on and found a space several seats away from us.

"I've got another name," Dotty said as the bus pulled away.

"Me too," I said. I had almost forgotten the great new name I had thought up during gym. "You go first."

"If your last name is Speaking, you shouldn't name your son Frank Lee."

"That's good. But I never heard of anybody named Speaking," I said.

"Sure, it's a good name. Now what's yours?"

"If your last name is Case," I said, "you shouldn't name your son Justin."

The bus made a stop and the kids on the seat behind us got out. Beagle quickly walked over and slid into the empty seat.

"I've got a name for you," he said.

"Hey, nobody's supposed to know about the name game," Dotty complained.

"The way you two go on everybody knows."

"It's okay," I said. "Tell us your name."

"If your last name is Count," Beagle said, "you shouldn't name your son Noah."

"Noah Count? I don't get it," Dotty said.

"Ya low-down, dirty, no-account, lying varmint," Beagle said in his worst western drawl. "No account, Noah Count, get it?"

"Yeah, I get it," Dotty said. We had just come to her stop, and she picked up her book bag and waved good-bye.

Beagle moved forward into her seat.

"I thought it must be bad news when the principal called you," I said. "But you seem to be in a good mood."

Beagle gave me a funny look.

"It couldn't be much worse," he said.

"What happened?"

"The principal doesn't believe anybody would do all this just to make me look guilty. He's convinced that I'm the one who wrecked the library. I guess it does sound dumb to say somebody is going to all this trouble to make me look bad. If I didn't know better, I'd probably think I did it too."

"But what did he want with you?"

"He warned me not to cause any more trouble, and he said he wasn't going to let me get away with the damage to the school. He intends to prove that I did it between the time I left the carnival and when your mother saw us on the sidewalk."

"But what about Mr. Shelby and Captain Holloway? Don't their opinions count?"

"He just thinks I have them fooled."

"What about your alibi? He can't get around that. You were with me."

"Oh, that's easy," Beagle said quietly. "He thinks you were my accomplice."

Unmasking
the Vandals ▣ **11** ▣

We had gotten off our bus and were standing on the roadside thinking about the problems facing us.

"You're always the one who says, 'We have a mystery to solve,'" I said. "Now it's my turn. We have to solve this thing once and for all, and we're going to start by finding out who vandalized the school. The only way we'll ever clear our names is by finding out who's really guilty."

"How?"

"The same way we solve every other mystery. First, we learn everything we can, and then we figure it out from there. Look, I already have some clues."

It didn't amount to much, but I had been making notes every time something had happened. Beagle took my notebook and read through the list.

"If your notes are right, Ellen, it looks like the vandals are eighth-graders," Beagle said.

"It's too bad we can't talk it over with Mr. Walters. The vandals probably left lots of clues in the library."

"This time we have a time limit. We need answers fast. Mr. Walters plans to take action this week. If we can't suggest anything better, he'll probably expel both of us."

Beagle and I studied my notes and made a list of suspects. Our suspects for the library wrecking turned out to be the same as my list of suspects for the egg-throwing.

"Okay, Ellen, we'll collect information and compare notes after school tomorrow," Beagle said when we were sure that we had learned all that we could for the moment.

I walked home thinking that this was going to be the worst case we had ever faced, and not just because there were too many suspects. *How are we ever going to talk to those guys?* I wondered.

I should have remembered that Beagle can talk to anybody. And the next day turned out to be full of surprises. A lot of the kids wanted to help us. Everybody had heard about the principal's suspicions, and the seventh-graders were mad.

"It's not any of us—it's *them*," I heard somebody say

on the bus, pointing toward the eighth-graders crowded together in the back.

Even Ricky wanted to help. He whispered, "Can I fight the bad guys with you?"

"How did you know about this?" I asked.

"Everybody's saying Beagle is in trouble. I like him. I think he's neat."

"Just keep your ears open and let me know if you hear anything about what happened at my school's library."

"I already heard something. Tyrone told Patty she should stay away from those two. And she said, 'Who do you mean?' And Tyrone said, 'I mean the two who wrecked the library.'"

I made a note of what Ricky had told me and thanked him. Help can come from unexpected places.

All the kids in our homeroom wanted to help. "They can't get away with this," they were saying.

Mr. Shelby let us discuss the problem right through homeroom period. Everybody agreed to report anything they could find out to me or Beagle.

"We'll help you find the real vandals," they said.

By the end of the day, I had stacks of notes. I didn't even try to speak to Beagle on the bus. There was just too much to say.

When we got off the bus, we headed for the shed

where we could sit at the desk and sort through the notes to see if any of them were helpful.

Our investigations showed that one of the suspects had destroyed the books while another stood guard. The suspects were Candace, Mac, Tyrone, Eric, Ken, Jenny, and Patty.

Below the names I listed the clues we found in our notes:

1. Candace and Ken had heard the vandal threatening to wreck the library.
2. Tyrone told Patty to stay away from the lookout and the vandal.
3. Candace said she would turn in the vandal if she could persuade Mr. Walters to excuse the lookout, who is her friend.
4. The vandal and Eric are both in Mrs. Moyer's homeroom.
5. The lookout and Ken were both suspended from school for three weeks last spring.
6. Eric and Mac are friends of the lookout's brother, who attends another school.

"Do you think we know enough to find out who's guilty?" Beagle asked.

"I don't know. Let's try it and see."

I drew a chart for all seven names, and Beagle and I began to fill in the information we had collected:

	lookout	vandal
CANDACE		
MAC		
TYRONE		
ERIC		
KEN		
JENNY		
PATTY		

[Help Ellen and Beagle clear their names by finding out who really damaged the school library. There are many suspects, so eliminate carefully. Remember that you are looking for two people, a lookout and a vandal.]

Solution to "Unmasking the Vandals":

Clue #1 eliminates Candace and Ken as the vandal. Tyrone and Patty are eliminated as both the lookout and the vandal by the second clue. Candace is not the lookout, according to the third clue. Eric can be eliminated as the vandal by clue #4. In clue #5, Ken is eliminated as the lookout. Eric and Mac are both eliminated as the lookout by clue #6. If you have been crossing off names on the chart, you will now see that there is only one person who can be the lookout, and that is Jenny. Once we know that Jenny must be the lookout, she is eliminated as the vandal. Therefore, Mac is the vandal.

Beagle and I went first to Mr. Shelby and explained everything we had learned. Mr. Shelby volunteered to go with us to present our case to Mr. Walters. Mr. Walters didn't really believe us at first, but at least he agreed to investigate. Before the day was over, he had proof that we were right.

By the next day everybody in school knew the truth. Mac had wrecked the library with the help of two high school boys, one of whom was Jenny's brother. Mac claimed he was getting revenge on Mrs. Ferguson, the school librarian, for all the times she had sent him to detention. But the funny thing was that Mac said he had never tried to pin the crime on Beagle, and none of the library vandals knew anything about the paint on Mr. Shelby's board.

"They couldn't be in worse trouble than they already are over the books they destroyed," I told Beagle. "I'm sure they're telling the truth about not spray-painting the chalkboard or drawing the picture of the beagle."

"Well, that's that," Beagle said. "At least we won't be expelled. But we still don't know who hates me—or why."

"Then that's our next problem, Beagle. We'll have to find out."

Beagle's
Secret Foe ◙ 12 ◙

In an effort to make up for his suspicions of Beagle, Mr. Walters let Beagle and me question Mac and Jenny in his office.

"Why me?" Beagle asked. "Why did you have to keep drawing beagles at the scene of every crime?"

"Look," Mac said, "we didn't try to pin it on you."

"He's telling the truth," Jenny told us. "There wasn't any drawing on the library door when we left."

"I don't get it," Beagle said when we left the principal's office. "Somebody drew a beagle on Mr. Shelby's board, but it wasn't the guy who owned the spray paint. Somebody drew a beagle on the library door, but it wasn't one of the same kids who wrecked the library."

"Oh, I don't think that's so hard to figure out," I said. "The person who's out to get you keeps trying to hide behind other people. But at least we know who our suspects are."

"Oh, yeah? Who?"

"The rest of Mac's crowd. They're the only ones who knew what was going to happen in the library. The person who threatened you at the Halloween carnival knew what was going to happen and had planned how he could use it to get you in trouble before Mac and his gang even got started."

"I think you're right," Beagle said. "And all of those five people ride our bus."

That afternoon on the bus we were still thinking about Beagle's secret enemy. We were almost home and the bus was half empty when Ricky came over and said, "I know a joke."

"So what's your joke?" I asked.

"If your last name is Bus," Ricky said, "you shouldn't name your child School."

Beagle and I both shook our heads.

"That's terrible," Beagle told him.

"Yeah." Ricky grinned. "I made it up."

When we got to our bus stop, I told Beagle I would

try to see him later. I wanted to do my homework, but there were also a couple of people I wanted to call. I thought I could pick up some more clues.

After supper, I made my phone calls and added to my list of clues. It didn't seem right to find the villain on my own. After all, this was Beagle's own puzzle. I took my clues to his house so we could solve it together. But I hadn't given Beagle enough credit.

At the shed, I found a note:

> ELLEN,
>   I know who it is. Ricky's joke got me thinking, and I worked it out. I've arranged a meeting back at the school.
>
>   BEAGLE

If your last name is Bus, you shouldn't name your child School. How could a dumb joke like that help to solve a mystery? Beagle had done it on his own. *He's changing*, I thought. Considering what a pain he has sometimes been, you'd think I would be glad to see him change. But all I felt was kind of let down.

Since he hadn't bothered to tell me the answer he had found, I went inside our detective agency and sat down at the desk to figure it out for myself. I looked

100

over the clues I had been saving to share with Beagle and drew up a chart:

Suspects: Candace, Eric, Ken, Patty, Tyrone.

1. Beagle's enemy tried to enlist the help of the one member of the group who has artistic talent, but the artist refused to be involved.
2. Eric knew that one member of their crowd hated Beagle but didn't realize how far things had gone.
3. Ken and Eric were both in Mr. Shelby's homeroom last year. The artist transferred to our school this year.
4. Patty and Tyrone, who have been students here for three years, were not aware of the plot against Beagle.

	artist	*Beagle's enemy*
CANDACE		
ERIC		
KEN		
PATTY		
TYRONE		

Studying the clues, I saw that I had enough information to solve the puzzle of who was behind all of Beagle's troubles. But when I found out *who,* there was no clue to tell me *why.*

[Using Ellen's clues, can you discover the name of Beagle's secret enemy? Check your answer against Ellen's on the next page.]

Solution to "Beagle's Secret Foe":

From clue #1, we learn that Beagle's enemy and the artist are two different people. Eric is not the enemy or the artist (clues #2 and #3). Clue #3 also eliminates Ken as the artist. Patty and Tyrone are both eliminated as the enemy in clue #4. Clues #3 and #4 together reveal that neither Patty nor Tyrone can be the artist, since we know from clue #3 that the artist is new at the school and from clue #4 that Patty and Tyrone have been there for three years. Now it is clear that only one person can be the artist, and that is Candace. Since she is the artist, Candace is not the enemy, which means that Ken is Beagle's secret enemy.

I was staring at the answer I had found when I realized all at once what Beagle had found out that I didn't know. I didn't know Ken's last name. The name game and Ricky's silly joke must have made Beagle wonder about the last names of our suspects. It was a guess on my part, but I was so sure I had to be right that the very next thing I was going to do was to find out Ken's last name.

I asked Beagle's mom if I could use their phone, and I called Mr. Shelby.

"Vernack," Mr. Shelby said in answer to my question. "Ken's last name is Vernack."

Vernack? I was puzzled until I remembered where I'd heard it before: Vernack was the name of the arsonist at the fairgrounds. Now that I knew, I was scared.

I was just about to ask Mr. Shelby to meet me at the school when I heard Beagle's voice behind me. I said a quick good-bye to Mr. Shelby and turned around to find Beagle raiding his refrigerator.

"What are you doing here?" I asked.

"Getting something to eat," he mumbled around a drumstick.

"No, I mean why aren't you at the school? What happened to your meeting with Ken?"

"That's set for tomorrow. I called and told him that I knew who he was and I wanted to see him. He said we'd settle it in the principal's office tomorrow during school. Huh! You didn't think I'd go without you?"

"What time?" I asked, ignoring his question because it was exactly what I had thought.

"He wouldn't say. He just said that I'd know and when I did to head straight for Mr. Walters' office. You'll come, won't you, Ellen?"

"Sure," I said, trying not to show how glad I was.

We waited all through the next day, and no signal came. I was beginning to think Ken had fooled us. Then, halfway through our last class of the day, the fire alarm went off. It was the first unusual thing that had happened all day.

"That's it!" Beagle whispered as Mrs. Lightner had us line up. "That's the signal."

We stayed with our class until we turned a corner in the hall. Then Beagle and I left the group.

We threaded our way through the halls until we reached the one leading to the principal's office and found it deserted. Everybody from the administrative office was helping to get students out of the building. Finding we were alone, Beagle broke into a run, and I followed as fast as I could. He also let out a battle yell, his fists punching the air as he trotted along.

Shouting and thundering along the hall, Beagle let his momentum carry him straight through the outer office and past Mr. Walters's door, which was just as well because he launched himself at Ken as soon as he saw him.

"Stop it!" Beagle cried.

I followed him into the office and saw that the room looked like a tornado had hit. Ken was using a steel bar to smash everything in sight.

"This time you won't weasel out," Ken told Beagle.

"When Mr. Walters gets back," I said, "you're the one who'll be in trouble."

"I'll be gone," Ken said. Struggling with Beagle, he had managed to twist himself around so that he was now between us and the only door into the room. "When I go out," he went on, "I'll lock the door behind me. It can only be opened with the key. You two will be caught red-handed. There's just one last thing to smash," he concluded, raising the metal bar and aiming it to hurl like a javelin into the control panel of the school's public address system.

"No, you don't," Beagle said, quickly stepping in front of the controls and spreading his arms out protectively as he faced Ken.

So far I'd been pretty useless, but an idea occurred to me. I threw myself beside Beagle, but I put my hands behind me.

I just had to hope that the big switch I had spotted was the right one to turn on the system for school-wide announcements.

"I don't understand this," I said, trying to hold Ken for a few more seconds. I could see through the window that people were already being moved back toward the doors.

"Look, Ken, can't we talk this over?" Beagle asked.

"I'm through talking, creep. Your dad's testimony will send my brother to jail. And, if it hadn't been for your snooping around the fairgrounds, he wouldn't have been caught at all."

Ken was almost shaking with anger. With luck, he would be concentrating so hard on ruining Beagle that he wouldn't hear the sounds that meant people were already pouring back into the building. I had a feeling that Beagle at least suspected that I had switched on the public address system because he tried to keep Ken talking.

"I didn't know Ron Vernack was your brother," Beagle said. "But arson is a serious crime."

"When they find the office torn apart," Ken said, "you won't be able to talk your way out of it because they'll find you too. It will look like you were getting even for Mr. Walters's suspicions when the door slipped and you were accidentally locked in. Now, step away from those controls."

"No," Beagle said.

Ken was stuck. One bruise on us would ruin his plan. He tossed the steel bar to the far side of the room, turned and quickly opened the door. Mr. Walters was standing on the other side.

"I think we've heard enough," he said as he came

through the door, marching Ken in front of him.

"It was Charles Beaghley," Ken said. "I caught him."

"Turning on the public address system was a smart move," Mr. Walters said, nodding to us. "Unfortunately for you, Ken, the whole school has been listening in."

Of course, it had been Ken who stole the spray paint and defaced Mr. Shelby's board. And it had been Ken who added the drawing of a beagle to the library door after Mac and his high school friends had finished there. And now it was Ken who had set off the fire alarm and then had torn apart the principal's office.

The bell was ringing for the end of the last class, and in a few moments Mr. Shelby joined us. He and Mr. Walters listened as we told the whole story, how Ken's older brother had lost his job at the fairgrounds, had set fires that burned two buildings and had almost gotten away with it, except that Beagle had insisted on lending the police a hand.

It was great to talk and have somebody listen. For the first time in months, Beagle was free of secret threats.

When the explanations were over, Beagle and I were glad to be able to leave the situation in Mr. Walters's hands. Once again we had missed the bus, and Beagle had to call his mom to pick us up.

A few minutes later we were riding along Center Street with Mrs. Beaghley when Beagle remarked confidently, "I know where we should be going next."

He has changed, I thought again. *He really sounds sure of where he's headed.*

"Where?" his mother asked.

"There," Beagle said, pointing to the giant, revolving doughnut sign above the Donut Shack just ahead of us.

On second thought, I decided, grinning, *he hasn't changed that much.*